Voices

from the

Valley

**Tales inspired by William Wordsworth's
*'The River Duddon, A Series of Sonnets'***

Stories by Fiona Pervez
Artwork by Barbara Wright

First published in 2021

© Fiona Pervez

ISBN: 978-1-913898-08-3

Artwork by © Barbara Wright

Book interior Design by Russell Holden

Pixel Tweaks Publications
SELF PUBLISHING MADE SIMPLE

www.pixeltweakspublications.com

For Caroline King

CONTENTS

WOLF HILL

'The Kirk of Ulpha to a pilgrim's eye
Is welcome as a star'
The Duddon Sonnets by William Wordsworth

Little is known of the exact age of 'the Kirk of Ulpha' but it has been thought that the first chapel-of-ease was situated near Ulpha Old Hall, when the Duddon Valley was densely forested. The presence of a church to administer spiritual guidance to the population, however sparse, was considered vital because in medieval times nearly everyone believed in God and heaven and hell.

The name 'Ulpha' is Old Norse for 'hill of wolves'. It is likely that in Ulpha, in medieval times, wolves outnumbered humans.

In 1281, Edward 1 (who died in Burgh on Sands, in Cumbria) ordered the total extermination of all wolves in England and the slaughter began. By the reign of Henry 11 (1489 - 1509), the ultimate predator at the top of the food chain was mostly eliminated, although folklore persisted. One story tells of the last killing of a wolf at Humphrey Head, Cark, in 1390, following attacks on sheep and a child.

However, the last reported killing of a wolf by a human does not necessarily mean that was the last wolf in the country. Wolves may have existed longer than we think, and if they did, Ulpha, in the Duddon Valley, would be a likely place.

The fearful reputation of the wolf lingers, yet, we can be drawn to them. Wolves and humans eat the same meat; sheep, cattle and deer.

They live in family units but have loners and leaders. They fight to keep territory but are prepared to travel. Family members baby-sit, play, show love, control the young and mourn the dead. Wolves and humans alike use body language to show submission or dominance.

This story of wolves and humans takes place in the thirteenth century in and around the Duddon Valley.

Chapter One

'Sun, moon, and stars, and beast of chase or prey'

The Duddon Sonnets by William Wordsworth.

Valdis was a lone wolf. Every day of winter he hunted but with poor results; the occasional rabbit snuffling under the snow for fallen bark, a frozen bird, and once, an early morning badger, poking his inquisitive nose from the sett.

If it wasn't for an injured deer, Valdis would have starved. The deer had struggled and kicked with an iron hoof, slashing the wolf's cheek to the bone with a well-aimed antler. Valdis had dragged the prey to his den and dropped, exhausted, to the ground. He did not have the strength to move for several days. But the meat from the deer sustained him until the winter days were over.

The white slash on Valdis' cheek never healed. The following winter, once more crazed by hunger, he became bold. He went near the largest human settlement he could find and waited for a chance to attack any living thing. People travelled in groups, for safety, and when they approached Egremont Castle they looked out for the wolf with the white scar. Valdis was a menace.

The young noblemen of that castle, brothers Eustace and Hubert de Lucie, each wanted to be the one to slay the wolf and bring home the trophy. But before they could do so, Valdis struck.

Following the early morning hunt, Eustace and Hubert rounded a bend to see the wolf poised on a huge rock. Valdis sprang, latching on to the back of Grunwilda, their uncle's wife. Unseating the young woman from her horse his powerful jaws ripped out her throat. The wolf would have dragged the body away, had not the brothers and other members of the hunt, chased it away with blades, rocks and sticks.

By slaying Grunwilde, Valdis had tasted human blood. The winter was not yet over; his coat was thin, his ribs showed through and his stores of energy were nearly gone. Hunger dominated his every move.

Eustace and Hubert knew there was nothing so deadly as a ravenous wolf. They hunted Valdis many times to avenge the death of Grunwilda but without success. Eventually they had to give up.

There was a more pressing obligation to fulfil: the Holy Land beckoned.

Chapter Two

'their turf drank purple from the veins
Of heroes fallen'

The Duddon Sonnets by William Wordsworth

The journey from England to the Holy Land was a dangerous undertaking; there was a one in twenty chance of survival. Even if they did complete the journey, crusaders faced death in battle. The elder brother, Eustace, made his will, as was the custom. Should he perish, the estate would pass to Hubert. But survive they both did, and once there, Eustace and Hubert faced the infidel with honour and courage.

The noble de Lucie brothers fought to the death. They completed their crusade and, covered in glory, looked forward to returning to the cool green lands of northern England. They prepared to come home.

For the younger brother, Hubert, there was one difficulty. As long as his elder brother, Sir Eustace, lived, the barony of Egremont was his and Hubert had nothing. Any dark hopes he had, that Eustace would fall in battle, had come to naught.

In the end, it was easily done. An agreement in the dead of night, a bag of gold with a promise of another, and Sir Eustace found himself captive and helpless in a dungeon.

"Fear not, brother," said the treacherous Hubert. "I will journey home to raise the ransom. You will be free ere long."

"It will take too long," said the despairing Eustace. "Even if you survive the journey. I fear I will be forgotten and left to die."

Indeed, by the time Hubert reached the family home, the memory of Eustace, chained half naked to a prison wall in a faraway land, had faded. There was much for the younger brother to see to; estates to manage, servants to supervise, a woman to wed and a family to raise. Brother Eustace, thought Hubert, had probably not survived his ordeal. Life must go on.

There was a respectable period of outward mourning, during which no news came from afar. Hubert decided it was time to assume the role of the Lord of Egremont.

"I am your lord now," he told the tenants and villagers. "You will pay your taxes to me and obey my laws. I will be the judge in all matters of dispute."

Being lord came easy to Hubert except for one thing; he could never banish the lingering guilt he felt about his brother. And there was one constant reminder of his treachery - a huge horn, which hung at the entrance of Egremont Castle. Sir Eustace had always said that the horn must never be blown by anyone other than the rightful Lord of Egremont.

The villagers and people who dwelt in the castle soon noticed that Hubert never blew the horn.

"Why does the master never blow the horn of Egremont?" they said. "He's the rightful lord, isn't he?"

They began to wonder.

Every time Hubert went through the castle gate, he cast his eyes elsewhere and never looked at the horn.

They noticed that too.

Chapter Three

'A dark plume fetch me from yon blasted yew,
Perched on whose top the Danish raven croaks;'

The Duddon Sonnets by William Wordsworth

After all his adventures in the Holy Land, Hubert had all but forgotten about the wolf with the white scar. But Valdis was a survivor too.

The wolf had endured the hardships of many a winter, but each spring, when the waters ran again and the animals came out of hibernation, his strength renewed. He was now a fierce predator and victor in many a fight.

By the time Hubert had returned from his crusades, Valdis had left the area around Egremont Castle and moved further afield. He ranged through thick forests until he found a mate and fathered cubs. Valdis and his wolf family lived in a part of the Duddon Valley known as Ulpha, the Hill of Wolves.

Valdis was leader of the pack and in his prime. Hubert was also a father and established as Lord of Egremont Castle. But what of the rightful lord, Sir Eustace?

He had suffered. For long years he was chained to a wall in a dark dungeon. He relied on the kindness of strangers for his food and water and waited for the return of his brother. And waited. When it became clear that Hubert would not be returning with a ransom, he expected that his life would soon be over.

'Your brother promised me more gold. He has proved himself to be an untrustworthy villain," the leader of the Muslim army said, in a fury. "He has betrayed me and because of that you must die."

He saw that Eustace's black hair had grown long during his years as a prisoner. "String him up by his hair," he ordered the guards. "And leave him."

Eustace prepared to die; he made his peace with the Almighty but his heart was overcome with sorrow at learning of his brother's treachery. The guards strung him up by the hair and shut the dungeon door. They thought he would be dead by morning.

But the Muslim leader was unaware that the young nobleman's fate was known to his daughter, a fair young maid by the name of Zaide. When she heard that he had been strung up by his hair, Zaide and her maid crept into the dungeon when the night was darkest. With a sharp knife, they cut the prisoner down by the roots of his hair. But, oh horror, in the dark and with fear and emotion, Zaide severed the skin, leaving the scalp suspended and bleeding.

Eustace survived the harrowing ordeal and, with the help of Zaide, escaped from the dungeon. One version of this story says that the beautiful Zaide accompanied his flight from the Holy Land, converted to Christianity and married him.

In any event, Eustace completed his journey and arrived home one summer's evening. He stood at the gate of Egremont Castle and wondered. Was his brother alive? Was he even now living in the castle? Eustace saw the horn and took it in his hands.

Inside, Hubert was seated at dinner with his wife and children. He watched as the servant brought his platter of wild boar and venison. He took up his goblet of wine and was about to drink when he heard a sound. The goblet clattered to the floor and Hubert threw back his chair.

'What is that noise? Who makes such a din?' he exclaimed, his face ashen.

Hubert knew very well what that sound was and who was making it.

The horn! His brother, Sir Eustace, was home. And his own presence in the dining hall, well fed, a husband and a father, proclaimed Lord of Egremont, was evidence enough of his guilt and treachery.

Shame flooded every fibre of Hubert's being. He knew he could never face his brother, the rightful Lord of Egremont Castle. Hubert ran out of the Great Hall and left by the postern gate. He gave not a backward glance, nor a passing thought to his wife and children.

Distraught at his own betrayal, his cowardice, and the abandonment of his family, but knowing he could never go back, Hubert wandered deep into the vast forests of birch, thorns and oaks. He avoided the bleak and barren hilltops and impassable morasses of fallen timber. He kept to the low woods, criss-crossed by numerous streams. He rambled for many miles, watched by sea eagles nesting high. Ravens and hawks followed him. He came to salt marshes alive with herons, wild duck and curlew; then he roamed the sands, home to fluke and cockles. He decided to follow the salmon upstream.

Finally he came to an area of the Duddon Valley known as Ulpha, the Hill of Wolves

Chapter Four

'as I cast my eyes,
I see what was, and is, and will abide;'

The Duddon Sonnets by William Wordsworth

Believing himself to be far away from the source of his disgrace and misery, Hubert found rough shelter and lived alone with his remorse and guilt. He came to know the little place of worship in Ulpha, where he prayed for forgiveness and lamented his sins.

Hubert's spirit was in torment. He thought himself unworthy of any comfort. He lived in rough conditions and welcomed hunger as a deserved punishment. He became as wild as any of the many animals that lived in the forest.

The golden months of summer and autumn turned to winter. The earth was caked in a thick frost and creatures disappeared to sleep until spring. Hubert was driven to a group of poor-looking dwellings in Ulpha. The occupants stood outside their homes of mud, stones, sticks and clay (wattle and daub) and watched as he approached.

"If I can sleep under your roof this winter," said the once proclaimed Lord of Egremont, "I'll help you work the land in the spring."

"You can sleep with the goat and share our pottage," said a man who spoke for the peasants. "We've paid our tithes to the church and last summer's harvest has all gone. There's nothing else left to eat."

The fight against cold and hunger was constant. Although there was place for a fire inside each dwelling, it was only lit for cooking the pottage. It was a time when people perished. Hubert saw that some may not survive the winter.

'But there's wood a-plenty,' he said. 'These vast forests are full of fallen timber.'

The villagers stared at him. They thought he was a holy man, a hermit with addled wits.

'I lost my son twelve months ago,' said Edda, cradling a new-born who was not expected to survive. 'To Millom gallows. For an armful of firewood and a pheasant. He'd not seen thirteen summers.'

Hubert was mortified. He, above all, knew the punishments for stealing from the lord of the manor; he had sent a man to the gallows himself. He looked at the villagers with new eyes, past their malnourished, poorly clad bodies and noticed their air of lethargy and defeat. No-one looked above thirty years. They had taken him in and sheltered him without knowing his true identity, without knowing his past.

His heart grew heavy. Hubert welcomed the harsh life of the villagers. He gave not a passing thought to the days when there would be a hog on a spit above a roaring fire at Egremont. He banished thoughts of his wife and children. In the darkest place of his mind, he suppressed the vision of his brother, chained and forgotten in a faraway land. He thought only of redemption and forgiveness.

Chapter Five

'*and here*
Declining manhood learns to note the sly
And sure encroachments of infirmity,
Thinking how fast time runs, life's end how near!'

The Duddon Sonnets by William Wordsworth

At this time, not far away, on the hillside lived five new-born wolf cubs. Tiny, blind and deaf, they knew only the smell of their mother and the yearning for her milk. In turn, their mother depended on her older cubs and the alpha male, Valdis, to bring meat to the den. Valdis had seen many winters but this one, with the late spring and early arrival of the latest cubs, was as desperate as he had known.

His memory took him to another time and place, when he had ventured near a human settlement. Cautious and cunning, he had not attacked travellers because they were always in groups. He had bided his time on a well-placed rock, his grey fur camouflaged and waited until a single rider turned the bend. Then he had leapt. The prey was so nearly his. He remembered the taste of human blood.

The memory drew Valdis once more to human habitation. On the first day, he loped around the outside of the village enclosure, dodging the rocks and stones they threw at him. On the second day, he skulked as light was breaking, pricking his ears to the feeble wail of a new-born. On the third day, he crouched on a large rock and waited. He could see no sign of the thing he most feared: fire. Then, the gate opened and through it came the solitary figure of a man.

Hubert's eyes flitted about as he walked out of the village enclosure. If there had been any firewood, he would have carried a lighted ember for protection. He sensed there were wolves nearby, their howls could be heard at night and they were getting closer.

But that was the reason he had ventured out; to gather fallen timber. He would take his chance and if he was sent to the gallows, so be it. He considered his life over, anyway. He was not going to spend another night wondering if Edda's baby would be found frozen to death, or if a wolf would make bold, enter the enclosure and snatch a child.

He had walked barely two minutes when Valdis leapt, baring his fangs. Man and wolf faced each other. Hubert saw the white wound on the wolf's cheek and he knew. This was the wolf that had slain his uncle's wife, all those years ago, in another lifetime at Egremont Castle. An image of hunting the wolf with his brother flashed before him. They had hunted this wolf together. They had gone to the Holy Land together. They were strong and courageous, seeking honour and glory together.

Hubert had no-one to blame but himself. Shame and self-recrimination overcame fear. Caring no longer for his own safety, he drew to his full height, raised his arms and let out a roar of pain and anguish. Let the wolf do its worst; it was no more than he deserved.

The noise drew the villagers who ran out with a clamour, shaking sticks and throwing stones. Valdis turned tail and fled.

His life spared, Hubert determined to do something good with it. He spent the day collecting wood and setting a trap for a boar. He gave the wood to the villagers and told them to check the trap the following day. He said he was going to the church at Ulpha, to confess, because he did not want anyone else to be punished for what he had done.

Then Hubert de Lucie made his way home, to Egremont Castle. When he reached the gate, he stopped to gaze at the horn.

Hubert passed through the gate and entered the Great Hall. He saw the familiar faces of servants and his brother seated at table. He walked into the centre of the room.

A silence fell on the Great Hall. Eustace turned to look at the stranger. There was something about the wretched and beggarly figure that made him stare.

The brothers faced each other across the dining hall.

"Hubert?" said Eustace.

All eyes in the company turned to Hubert. There was a murmuring and then a silence.

"I seek your forgiveness, brother," said Hubert. "I am guilty of many sins, but above all, of plotting your demise. I am not worthy to live. I am here to throw myself at your mercy. I will take any punishment you deem fit." He fell to his knees.

Sir Eustace stood, a figure of authority. His wounds had healed and he was the respected Lord of Egremont. He looked at the bedraggled and pitiful form of his brother.

"Cast your eyes on this,' said Sir Eustace, pointing. 'I look upon it every day. It reminds me of my faithless brother and the torture I endured."

Hubert stared at the scalp, hanging from a beam by long black hair.

"I brought this back from the Holy Land. So that I would never forget what I suffered because of you. Every day since I returned, my hatred for you is kept alive by the sight of this thing. But now I see you before me and the hatred in my heart has gone. I remember only the times we shared as boys and the bond between brothers."

Hubert bowed his head and wept.

"I am the Lord here," said Sir Eustace, "so it befits me to be gracious. Come, brother and let bygones be bygones."

The brothers reconciled. And Sir Eustace, to show faith in his brother's new found goodness, offered Hubert the manor of Millom.

So it was that Hubert and his family went to live in Millom Castle, at the foot of the Duddon Valley. Hubert was humbled by his brother's forgiveness and sincerely contrite. He determined to do good in the time he had left on earth. He turned a blind eye to smoke coming from up the valley and allowed the villagers to fish. While he was there, the gallows fell into disuse.

Footnote

The old Hudleston crest of Millom Castle is that of a bloodied scalp, held aloft by two arms clad in chain-mail. The story is referred to as 'The Horn and the Hatterel' (scalp) as told in 'The Legend of the Crest' by Annette Hudleston Harwood.

Millom gallows stood near the castle. A large stone was placed on the spot and bore the inscription (now worn away by the elements) 'on this spot stood a Gallows the ancient lords of Millom having exercised Jura Regalia within their seigniory'

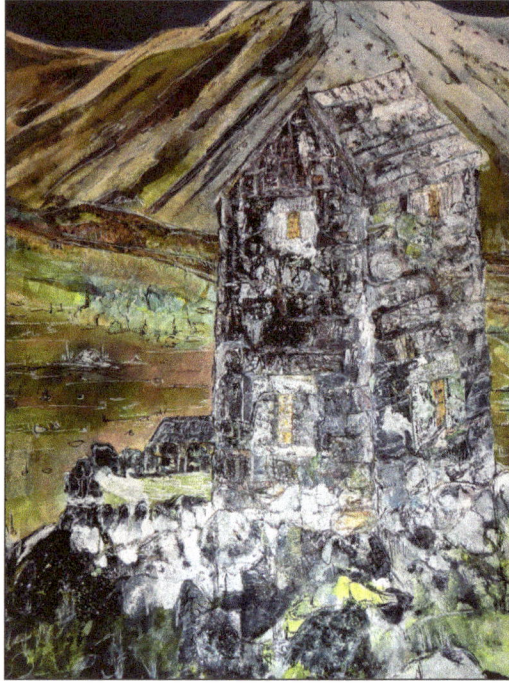

   Ulpha Old Hall, near Holehouse Gill, is sometimes described as a ruined, sixteenth century pele tower. Legend says the Lady of the Hall was drowned while fleeing from a wolf. The place where she reportedly drowned is known as 'Lady's Dub', a deep pool in a ravine.

BECKSTONES

'Was it by mortals sculptured?'

The Duddon Sonnets by William Wordsworth

'From the first I have been a simple communicator using plain form as Wordsworth used plain words.'

Josefina de Vasconcellos

Josefina de Vasconcellos, daughter of a Brazilian diplomat, was a well-connected and acclaimed sculptor. She worked in stone, bronze, wood, lead and perspex. In 1948 she became the first female fellow of the Royal British Society of Sculptors. Her artist husband, Delmar Banner, painted landscapes but his most well-known work is a portrait of Beatrix Potter which hangs in the National Portrait Gallery.

Sculpture was not Josefina's only passion; she was to become the driving force behind several schemes to encourage children to appreciate the natural world. In the mid 1960's she chose Beckstones in the Duddon valley as the location for one of her projects; an outward-bound centre for youngsters.

The story leading up to Josefina's association with Beckstones, begins in the Second World War.

In 1939 Josefina and her husband moved to The Bield in Little Langdale. In 1941 Beatrix Potter, now a friend, wrote to Josefina stating, 'German planes go over on passage elsewhere and sometimes unload their bombs'. The Luftwaffe flew over the Lake District on the way back from Barrow-in-Furness, after targeting the shipyard and the steelworks. A remote farmhouse took one such bomb, killing a farmer, his wife, mother, two children, a maidservant and five evacuees. The Lake District may have appeared picturesque and peaceful, but it did not escape bombs and aircraft disasters.

Despite the returning Luftwaffe, The Bield provided a welcome haven for many friends, (including artists from the Royal College of Art, which had been re-located to nearby Ambleside).

One esteemed friend of the artistic couple, Ronald Edmond Balfour, was an academic and historian from King's College Cambridge. His specialities were manuscripts, books of worth and historical papers.

In April 1940, Ronald Balfour rescued two motherless boys from a burning building in the centre of London and brought them to The Bield. He asked Josefina and Delmar to 'do their bit for the war' by looking after them. Within weeks, the boys were speaking broad Cumbrian and it was not long before Josefina and Delmar adopted the boys legally. Billy and Brian were enrolled in the local school and their family life began. Ronald Balfour continued to visit The Bield during the war years and Billy and Brian became fond of him, knowing him as 'Uncle Ronald'.

In 1944 Ronald Balfour began work with the Monuments, Fine Arts and Archives section (MFAA) of the Supreme Headquarters Allied Expeditionary Force. He was one of the Monuments Men[1], a group of archivists, artists,

---

1 The **Monuments Men** was a group of soldiers whose aim was to assess combat damage to buildings and to retrieve cultural items and works of art that had been stolen during the Nazi occupation of Europe. Over five million works of art had been seized and transported to the Third Reich. About the time Ronald Balfour was killed, there were sixty or so Monuments Men, mostly American or British.

The story of how the Monuments Men went to Germany to rescue masterpieces and return them to the rightful owners is depicted in the 2014 film 'The Monuments Men' starring George Clooney. In the film, Ronald Balfour is loosely portrayed by Hugh Bonneville.

Work on retrieving stolen art and restoring them to their original owners continues. The Commission for Looted Art in Europe was set up in 1999. In 2006, a painting was returned to its original owner, a gallery in Berlin, by the BBC journalist and broadcaster, Sir Charles Wheeler. It had been given to him as a wedding present in 1952 and had been absent since 1944.

architects, curators and museum directors whose job it was to retrieve works of art that had been stolen by Nazi Germany.

Tragically, while attached to the Canadian Army, Ronald Balfour was killed in 1945, by a shell-burst in the German town of Cleves. He was in the process of preserving historic church artefacts. It was a grievous loss to his family and friends, and a bitter blow to the MFAA team. His knowledge of historical books and papers was unmatched.

News of the death of Ronald Balfour eventually made its way to The Bield and was the inspiration for Josefina's sculpture 'The Hand', worked in Honister green slate. Her tribute was given to St Bees School and dedicated as a war memorial in 1955.

Ronald Balfour's legacy lived on in the lives of Billy and Brian. Their circumstances had kindled Josefina's interest in the plight of abandoned, neglected children and she planned to act upon it.

In 1955 Josefina worked with boys from twenty-one approved schools to set up an exhibition in the crypt of St. Paul's Cathedral (Mary and Child). The boys and Josefina worked well together and the scheme was a success. Works in other towns and cities followed.

Later, in 1959 boys from the probation home (run by the London Police Court Mission) helped her with a sculpture entitled 'They Fled by Night'. This was exhibited at the church of St Martin-in-the-Fields, Trafalgar Square and later given to Cartmel Priory.

While sculpting in her garden in the summer of 1964 Josefina became aware of a group of boys peering over the wall, watching her, engrossed. They were on an outdoors expedition with their teacher and enjoying the chance to experience the natural world. Josefina, having strong religious convictions, believed in redemption and rehabilitation and the healing power of nature. She knew then what her next project would be.

Supported by her friend Norman Nicholson, Josefina called on other influential friends to become involved in her project. With the guidance of the Church of England Council for Social Aid and the children's department of the Home Office, a committee was formed. Lord Denning was the trustee and the Bishop of Norwich the president. The Bishop of Carlisle was patron and Reverend Austen Williams from St. Martin-in-the Fields took the chair.

The perfect place, they found, was Beckstones, a dilapidated ruin in the Duddon Valley which had stood empty for nearly thirty years. The committee obtained a peppercorn rent from the owner, the National Trust, and work on its restoration began. The first working party came from Castle Howard and the boys' initial task was to chop down a sycamore tree that was growing in the centre of the building. Pelham school in Calderbridge soon followed and by 1967 boys and their teachers had come from all over the country to make Beckstones habitable.

The scheme caught the imagination of the national press and the *Times Educational Supplement* published a comprehensive article in support of the concept. Working parties from the Duke of Edinburgh Awards and the International Voluntary Service contributed. Josefina was seeing a cherished dream come to reality.

By 1968 Beckstones Outward Bound Centre was up and running. The building was restored to its original appearance and named 'Outpost Emmaus' after the biblical story of renewed hope.

Josefina never forgot the fate of those who had lost their lives in plane crashes on the fells. One tragedy haunted her: the image of corpses in their parachute harnesses, dangling upside down on the icy crags. The young men had bailed out of the aircraft and the wind had taken them. She dedicated Beckstones chapel to their memory. The ceremony was attended by representatives of the Royal Air Force Northern Command. The vicar of Seathwaite and Ulpha, the Rev Roy Greenwood, a Himalayan climber, became chaplain.

Although Josefina considered the chapel an important part of Beckstones life, she did not want the children to feel that attending chapel was being forced upon them. She made it accessible to all and open to the elements, with no door and swallows nesting in the eaves. The ancient altar had been brought from St. Martin-in-the-Fields and she had constructed the cross from pitons and ice-axes.

The Beckstones Centre was a success. Many childrens, teachers, supporters and friends had happy times there, learning skills and enjoying the beautiful countryside.

After several happy and fulfilling years, in 1980 the lease on Beckstones was due to expire. There were few bookings and no warden, and so the building once more became the property of the National Trust. The altar was returned to St Martin-in-the-Fields.

In 1984, a year after Delmar died, Josefina received the MBE for 'Services to the Community in Cumbria'. By this time, she was involved in the Harriett Trust Outdoor Centre, a converted fishing trawler on the Duddon Estuary which catered for people with disabilities. This project lasted until 1998. Josefina continued to lead a fulfilling life until her death in 2005, just after her 100th birthday.

Her sculpture 'Reconciliation', commissioned by Sir Richard Branson, marked the 50th anniversary of World War II. Bronze casts were sited in Coventry Cathedral, Hiroshima Peace Park, the Berlin Wall and Stormont Castle, Belfast. Josefina's work can be found in many establishments.

Josefina's portrait sculptures include Norman Nicholson, Sir Roger Bannister, Edith Sitwell and Tenzing Norgay. In addition, she wrote a book about her friend, Beatrix Potter (*She was Loved: Memories of Beatrix Potter* Publisher Titus Wilson).

In later years, Josefina de Vasconcellos was the oldest living sculptor in the world.

Beckstones is now a climbing hut.

FRITH (IN-THE-WOOD) HALL

Chapter One

'lowly is the mast
That rises here, and humbly spread the sail;'

The Duddon Sonnets by William Wordsworth

"I think I've been poisoned," groaned Ralph. He grabbed the rail and threw up over the side of the boat. The wind caught it and blew it back in his face.

"Aargh," he spluttered, wiping his face with his sleeve. "Gimme some water, quick."

At that moment the vessel gave a violent lurch and a huge wave crashed on deck, nearly knocking Ralph over. He staggered backwards, dripping wet.

"Well, you did ask for water," said his friend Jake, who thought it was funny.

Ralph took a deep breath. He was about to say something very rude when he noticed a figure looming out of the darkness. His heart sank. It was the gang-master. In daytime the gang-master wore an eye-patch. He believed it would help him to see in the dark. But now, at night, it was pushed up on his forehead. He carried a pistol in his belt and a bottle of rum in his hand.

"You're not on some little fishing boat now lads," the gang-master said, looking at the bedraggled Ralph. "This is my very fine lugger.

You'll soon get your sea legs and learn not to throw up in the wind. Stop complaining before I send you up my splendid rigging." He took a swig of rum.

"Yes sir, sorry sir," said Ralph, holding on to the rail and trying to ignore his queasy stomach. For as long as he could remember, he'd wanted to join the Isle of Man's smuggling gang. Finally, after years of trying to get noticed, he had been given a chance. This isn't the impression I wanted to give, thought Ralph. Dripping wet and covered in sick. He caught a whiff of the rum and threw up again.

"You've got guts coming on this venture, I'll say that for you," said the gang-master. "Shame you're puking them up all over the place." He walked off, laughing.

The lugger rolled and surged. Ralph put his head between his knees and gave a long moan. "We must be nearly there by now," said Jake. "But we'll have to help unload. No kip for us tonight."

"I'll just be glad to feel dry land under my boots. Nothing can be worse than this," said Ralph. He looked at Jake. "We've never been this far away from home before. They say where we're going is a God-forsaken place full of evil spirits. Do you think it's true?"

"Probably," grinned Jake. "But no worse than back home."

They heard voices. "The spotsman's sending a signal to land," Ralph realised. "We're here."

"What happens now?" asked Jake.

Ralph knew. He'd heard about it so many times. "We watch out for an answering signal from the coast. If there's no light that means preventive officers are on the prowl and we can't go ashore. Because if they catch us, they'll arrest us. But, if we do see a light, then the coast is clear. We can drop anchor and start unloading."

"How do we know we're in the right place?" asked Jake. They'd been sailing for hours.

"The gang-master knows what he's doing," said Ralph. "Finding the right place is the easy bit. It's getting caught that's the problem. But the ship's painted black and the sails are black. We can't be seen on a moonless night like tonight. And our friends will be looking out for us."

Everyone was peering into the darkness. The lugger's violent lurching subsided.

"Yes, there it is. A light! We're all set. The coast is clear."

"All hands on deck," ordered the gang-master, "but keep your voices down."

Ralph and Jake grabbed some tobacco bales wrapped in oilskins and threw them into the sea. They unloaded barrels and rolled them along the deck.

"Heave-ho," grunted Jake as they hoisted each one overboard. Ralph watched the barrels bob up and down on the waves until shadowy figures appeared and dragged them to land. More goods were taken away in rowing boats. Men spoke in undertones, the sound of the sea drowning out their voices.

"I can't wait to get off this ship," muttered Ralph. He climbed over the rail and jumped, legs flailing in the darkness. There was a loud splash. The shock of the cold sea revived him. At least I won't stink of vomit now, he thought, spitting out the salty water. It's good to be off that ship. Jake followed and the two lads scrambled ashore.

The gang split into two groups; 'tub-men', who carried the kegs, and 'bat-men' who were there as a look out for the preventive officers. If any were spotted, there would be fierce fighting. Smugglers were desperate to keep the goods and avoid the law.

The gang-master adjusted his patch and turned his attention to the two young boys. He's got a glare that could pierce a rock, Ralph thought.

"Listen up," said the gang-master. "The local squire is the venturer. He's put up the money for this contraband and he's expecting to make a profit. We'll be using his horses. And men from his land. A lot of the liquor's going up the Duddon Valley to Frith Hall. And you two are going with it."

"All the way up the valley?" Ralph frowned, thinking of his weak legs. "Isn't there anywhere nearer we can leave it?"

The gang-master grabbed Ralph by the collar and shook him until he was nearly sick again.

"Stop interrupting, you insolent fool," he said through gritted teeth. "It's not your place to ask questions. You're here to follow my orders. One mistake and we're done for. I'm giving you a chance here. Don't make me live to regret it."

"Yes sir. Sorry."

"Shut up. If you get this wrong, it'll be the worse for you." He took a deep breath and resumed. "Frith Hall, that's where you're taking the contraband. You'll have a guide. He'll lead the horses. Follow him up the Duddon estuary and past an old castle. Skirt round the ruin and go through the woods. There's a bridle path. Then it's over the fell until you get to Frith Hall. You'll soon get to know the ropes. That's why I'm sending you. To learn."

He paused and eyed them sternly. "This journey is dangerous. The ground will be muddy and boggy in places, but with any luck there'll be a frost and that makes it easier going. The woods will be dense and difficult to walk through. Nearly all your walking has to be done at night. You rest during the day. As well as that, you have to watch out for signs of preventive officers lurking around. They will arrest you and drag you off to the gallows before you can say knife. We don't know how many work in this area, but there will be some. And we know there are gallows at Millom, so don't let your guard down. Ever."

He paused. "But there's something else, too. Could be the most dangerous of all. Somewhere on the fells lives a man who wants a cut of everything. He's a robber, a bandit. This villain will use a weapon and take what he can. So, you have to be on the look-out for him as well as the officers. He will know that Frith Hall is due a drop off. No doubt he's threatened somebody at knife point to get as much information he can. I know he's killed before and one of these days......" The gang-master broke off, a faraway look in his eyes.

Ralph stared. He knew smuggling involved a lot of subterfuge and secrecy. He knew about the excise men and preventive officers. But wasn't it only the gang-leaders that got sent to the gallows, not boys like himself and Jake? And what about this murderer roaming the fells? They had no chance if they met up with him. Ralph shuddered. He was still soaked from jumping in the ocean, and weak from being so sick.

"But you have two advantages," continued the gang-master. "One is that this rogue does not know exactly when the drop off will be. So, you can be on your guard. The other is that you will know who he is if you meet him, because the fingertips on his right hand are missing. He chopped them off himself when his hand got trapped under a fall of boulders. He was making a cave to hide away his stolen goods and there was a landfall. Serves him right."

The gang-master grimaced and hitched his belt.

"Last of all, look out for the signal from Frith Hall that tells you there is no-one around. But don't take it for granted. Keep your wits about you and listen for anything out of the ordinary. The signal is three candles, lit one after the other. One, then two, then three, so there are three candles

burning at the same time in the window. When the third candle is lit, it's all clear and you can unload the goods into the barn. When everything is unloaded, give a long low whistle. Someone will be listening for it. Then leave."

He nodded in the direction of a line of horses, with the shadowy outline of a man standing at the front.

"Them's your horses. Twelve in all. When you pass a building, bind all four hooves of each horse with these rags, to muffle the sound. And here's your load," he said, pointing. "Make sure the weight is even on both sides. When you've unloaded the goods at Frith Hall, bring the horses straight back to this very same place. The squire's man will take them back. Four nights travelling, not including tonight, and on the fifth night, we leave. Get back here and watch out for a signal from the ship. A lantern. You'll have to wade out to get yourselves on board. There'll be no rowing boat. Make sure you make it. Otherwise, we leave without you."

He held their gaze for several long seconds. "The best advice is this; do not let anyone see you or hear you. If everything goes as it should, you'll be paid with tea and brandy. Yours to drink or sell or whatever. Maybe a guinea between you if you do a good job. I'll take my leave. I've got another drop to make further up the coast."

He turned his back and left.

Chapter Two

'And through this wilderness a passage cleave'

The Duddon Sonnets by William Wordsworth

Ralph blew out his cheeks and stretched his eyes. He looked at Jake, who shrugged a response.

A large figure leading a line of horses emerged from the darkness. "Name's Ben," said a rough voice. "Am gonna tek ye to Frith. We'll be reet but it's a long trek. Let's git garn. And na yattering."

Jake stared.

"Let's get going. And no talking." Ralph guessed. We're in the north of England now, not the Isle of Man."

They set off in the calm, moonless night. Ben led the first pack horse, with Ralph in the middle of the line and Jake bringing up the rear. It was still dark and they knew better than to speak. Ralph recognised a familiar feeling in his stomach. Hunger. It would be water and dry biscuits for a few days yet.

"Don't let anyone see you," the gang-master had said. But Ralph sensed he was being watched. Suddenly, a white face appeared in the dark, accompanied by a rhythmic beating. But, no, that was an owl, following them upstream.

"Don't cross my path," said Ralph beneath his breath. "I don't want bad luck tonight."

The owl screeched and landed on a nearby branch.

The thought of the grim penalty for being caught with pack horses laden with brandy and rum stayed in Ralph's mind. But like everyone else on the Isle of Man, he saw smuggling as a crime invented by the government. The goods were bought and paid for, not stolen. The right to buy and sell was freedom of choice. Of course, the government missed out on the taxes they wanted to collect. But who cared about the greedy government wanting more money?

What else were ordinary folk to do? Ralph knew that Jake thought the same. Almost everyone on the Isle of Man was involved in the illegal trade; old people kept a look-out, young people carried the contraband, and fishermen and sailors arranged transport. Villagers all closed their shutters at night and turned deaf ears to the clip-clop of horses, low whistles and hushed voices.

But accompanying a train of pack horses laden with contraband was the most dangerous part of smuggling. If a preventive officer was hiding behind the next bush, nothing would save them.

They trudged on. The ruins of a castle came into view as a watery sun started to rise.

Ben stopped his horse and turned round to look at the other two. In the dawn, the three saw each other's faces clearly.

He's about our age, thought Jake. But bigger and wider.

He looks older than us, thought Ralph. I wouldn't want to get on the wrong side of him.

They're nobbut bairns, thought Ben. They'd better mind what Ah say. Ah'm in charge here. They better know it.

"Yon's old Millom Castle, Ben informed them. "We canna stop here, someone may chance by." He kept his voice low but with an air of authority. "Castle's been deserted since Cromwell's lot beat the lord. Had to scarper, he did, lord whate'er-his-name-was. But that was aboot a hundred years ago. 1644, they reckon. No-one's lived here since. 'Cepting 'obs, of course."

"'obs?" asked Jake.

"'obgoblins. Divn't ye ken?"

I can tell I'm far from home, thought Ralph. He looked at the damaged walls and the cannonballs still littering the ground. The steps were mossy and neglected. Timber creaked and the wind whistled through the gaps in the walls.

It's going to rack and ruin, Ralph thought. There's probably a ghost as well as 'obs, or whatever Ben said. Nobody's ever going to live here again. He thought he felt a hand on his shoulder and turned around. No-one. A movement of a shadow on the castle steps caught his eye. The shape shifted and evaporated. Ralph shivered. A horse nearby whinnied.

Ben carried on walking. Fallen branches and upturned roots made their progress slow. Ralph stumbled and turned his ankle. He limped, holding on to a saddlebag for support. He couldn't get left behind.

"We'll unload an' rest here awhile," said Ben, as they came to a clearing. "Yer two can tek the horses to watter. Tether 'em when ye fetch 'em back. Ah's garn yonder fer a kip."

What did your last servant die of? Jake wanted to know.

By the time they could feel the sun's weak warmth, the two boys had wrapped themselves in horse blankets and chosen a spot to lie down. The turf was soft and springy under the trees on the edge of the clearing. Tired out, all three fell asleep to the comforting sound of horses chomping.

Chapter Three

'Or, near that mystic round of Druid frame
Tardily sinking by its proper weight
Deep into patient earth, from whose smooth breast it came!'

The Duddon Sonnets by William Wordsworth

Ralph woke late afternoon. He saw Ben, sitting with his back against a tree, munching.

"What are you eating?" asked Ralph, his stomach rumbling.

"Yonder's a clump of wood sorrel growing wild. An' there's a pile of beech nuts that the boggarts left. They must have ken we were coming. I brought me own bread," he added, not offering to share.

"Thank you," said Ralph. He would try anything. He started to walk over to where Ben had pointed. "But what are boggarts?"

"The wee folk. Don't you have 'obs and boggarts where you come from? There's a lot roond 'ere. In the summer they make circles out of la'al white mushrooms. You can see rainbow lights and hear singing. But never go inside the circle. You'll get carried away to a dark place." Ben tore off another piece of bread.

32

"Boggarts and 'obs," said Ralph. "If you're trying to scare us with stories of spirits in the other world, you'll have to try harder."

"Oomph." A thud and Ralph found himself lying face down in the grass, his face inches away from a pile of horse manure.

"What did you do that for?" he said, annoyed. "What's the matter with you?" He looked at Ben, who hadn't moved, and was still sitting with his back against the tree, totally unsurprised to see Ralph full length on the ground. Jake, still dazed from sleep, was getting to his feet.

"Boggarts divn't take kindly to non-believers," said Ben. "Jus' watch out what you say around here."

Ralph was irritated. He was cold and hungry and still had a sore ankle. There was another day's hard slog ahead and he was tired of Ben's stories.

"Boggarts. Bah!"

"Load up and less get garn," said Ben, as soon as Jake was on his feet. "We've got a schedule. An' muss stick to it."

They set off again, their eyes becoming accustomed to the declining daylight.

It's warmer when we're on the move, Ralph thought. The air was frosty, and the ground was hard with tiny rivulets of frozen water, that crunched and splintered under their feet. They stopped three or four times, to bind the horses' hooves with rags. Ben put his finger to his lips as a warning not to utter a single word, and they passed the dwellings as silently as they could. If they were heard, no-one let on.

The night passed uneventfully. They knew they were coming near a farm when a stray piglet, rooting in the undergrowth, squealed and bolted. They came out of another wooded area into the lightness of dawn. There was a faint outline of a track, bordered by a ditch on one side and grass covered ridges on the other.

Ralph stopped, gazing ahead. He turned round to Jake and pointed. "Giants!" he mouthed.

Jake frowned into the distance He could see large shapes gathered in a circle.

Ben carried on leading the train of packhorses, unaware of Jake and Ralph's interest. He had passed the stone circle many times. It was just an old stone circle. They said it had been there since the beginning of time.

As they got closer, Ralph and Jake realised that the stones were not giants but huge boulders, bigger than the biggest of men. The stones hunkered and stooped alongside each other; immovable and solid in a crooked circle, too many to count.

That's an impressive stone circle, thought Ralph. I'm going nearer to get a better look, see what it's like in the middle. He motioned his intentions to Jake, then left the train of packhorses and dodged behind the nearest large stone, just in case Ben glanced back.

A few seconds won't harm, thought Ralph. He limped into the circle with the warmth of the rising sun in his face. The huge stones threw long shadows before them.

But as soon as he reached the centre of the circle, Ralph sensed something strange was happening. The shadows started to twist and curl, taking on human forms. The figures began a rhythmic movement, heads nodding

and feet stamping. Ralph watched in dread fascination as a face formed on one of the stones and stared at him.

Ralph backed away from the centre of the circle, face white, eyes stretched.

"Aargh!" he exclaimed. He had backed into a stone and banged his head. He felt a movement behind him and turned, alarmed. The stone was growling, vibrating.

"Do excuse me," said Ralph to the stone. He ran out of the circle and straight into a preventive officer.

Chapter Four

'a shadow large and cold'

The Duddon Sonnets by William Wordsworth

"How considerate of you to detach yourself from your fellow smugglers and present yourself to the law," said the preventive officer with a sneer. "I've been following you since Millom Castle but I can't manage three arrests on my own. I'm going to tie you up, leave you in the nearest barn and force the farmer to come with me for the others. The magistrate can deal with the lot of you when the time comes."

Ralph stumbled backwards in shock and fear. He had much ado to gather his wits. If he was arrested now, he couldn't warn the others. They would be caught too. Their chances of going home would be nil. Gaol and the gallows loomed. It would be the end of everything, his life too, probably. But, he realised, the preventive officer did not know what Ralph knew about the stone circle.

"Don't think you can run away," said the officer, following Ralph, who was backing into the circle. "I saw you limping. If you come quietly, you can hope for a lenient sentence. Maybe deportation instead of hanging." He grinned. His teeth were either rotting or missing.

"It's about time some of you lot faced justice, always giving us the runaround. One day I'll capture that lugger and the one-eyed rascal who runs it. Then I'll cut the boat to pieces and watch your precious gang-master dance at the end of a rope."

He lunged at Ralph and brought him down with a vicious thud, rolling him over and forcing his arms behind his back. Ralph struggled at first, then lay still. He could see the shadows creeping towards him.

"That's it. May as well make it easy for the both of us," the preventive officer said, starting to tie Ralph's hands together. The creeping shadows took on their human forms. The air crackled like a thunderstorm. The officer stopped what he was doing and looked about. He got to his feet and spun round wildly.

Yes, thought Ralph. I know how you feel.

"What's this? What is it?" He looked at the nearest stone. "Whose face is that? In the name of all that's holy, I know that face." He dropped the rope. "No, no! he bellowed. "Not you! It can't be. It's not possible.". With a loud wail, he ran out of the circle.

Ralph lay still, then wriggled his hands free and gathered the rope in one hand. He got to his knees and slowly stood up. He wound the rope four or five times around his waist and knotted it. The raging continued and the images and shadows were just as threatening as before. But Ralph knew they would stop as soon as he left the circle. So, he left the circle.

He ran, cursing his sore ankle, and caught up with the packhorses, Jake still at the rear. He took his place in the centre of the line, as though he had never left, and grabbed a saddlebag and hung on. He was panting and his legs felt wobbly, like they did on the ship. Had he really escaped from a preventive officer? He had been so nearly arrested. And what were all those shadows and faces?

Jake had been watching for his friend's return. Something's up, he thought. Ralph's legs are shaking like he's an old man. And where did that rope come from? Jake didn't remember that. It made him anxious. The first chance he got, he would ask Ralph what happened back there, in the circle of stones.

Ralph took some deep breaths and steadied himself. Well, there's one thing for sure, he thought. What happened in the circle wasn't my imagination.

That officer proved it. He didn't hang about. He ran away screaming. And not in our direction either. With any luck, he won't come back. I hope we've seen the last of him.

Ralph wondered whose face the officer thought he saw. Then he remembered he had excused himself to a stone. How foolish he felt now. It was all too much to think about. Ben, glancing back, saw nothing amiss. He had not noticed Ralph's sudden detour into the stone circle and of course was unaware of the appearance of the preventive officer. He did think, though, that Ralph was looking a bit paler than before.

A raven cawed and flew to a nearby crag. An eagle circled overhead as they crossed a pack horse bridge.

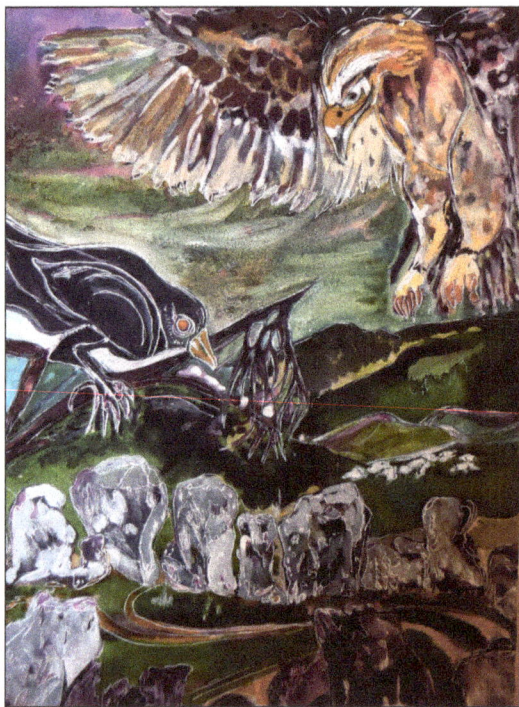

"What was that circle of big boulders we passed?" Ralph asked Ben, when they had stopped to let the horses drink from a nearby stream and when it was safe to talk.

"They tried to build a church there years ago but the de'il kept pulling it darn at night," Ben replied. "Those styans are all what's left. They call it Sunkenkirk."

Jake and Ralph exchanged glances and smiled. It reminded them of Meayll Circle on the Isle of Man where they played as boys.

"'obs and boggarts and now the devil," said Jake. "Are you superstitious by any chance?"

"Tha'll learn," said Ben. "Tha's the way life is roond here. Follow me and let's get to Swinside Farm. They'll be up by now, but it canna be helped. They'll hear us coming and turn away to face the wall. That way they can honestly say they haven't seen us. There's a barn further on. Mebbe we'll rest there for the day."

Ralph decided not to tell Ben about the preventive officer just yet. He felt sure there was not going to be another appearance from the law anytime soon. And he didn't want Ben to know that he'd left the line of packhorses, even if it was for just a few minutes.

I expect Ben would believe what happened in the circle, though, Ralph thought. He believes everything else.

Ralph thoughts returned to his stomach. He envied the horses; all they wanted was grass and water and there was plenty of both.

"Will there be food left out for us in the barn?" he asked.

Ben did not reply. He got to his feet; eyes fixed in the distance. He held up a hand.

"Whisht," he said, and pointed.

Chapter Five

'Rough ways my steps have trod'

The Duddon Sonnets by William Wordsworth

Above the fells, in the distance, there was a very faint, but undeniable, trace of smoke.

"Frith Hall?" asked Jake, hopefully.

"Nah," replied Ben. "Thart's too close. And it's the wrong direction for Fenwick's farm as weel. That fire's o'er by Penn Mountain. There's an old derelict homestead there. It's ancient and there's no roof. Ah wonder."

"The man with chopped-off fingers?" suggested Ralph.

"More than likely," said Ben. "Although ye never ken for sure where he is until e's got a knife at yer throat."

"Could be just a poacher," shrugged Ralph.

"Poachers divn't give the game away with a plume of smoke," Ben said, with impatience." Poaching is as bad as smuggling, in the eyes of the law. It looks like a signal for something. Hmm. Well, there's nowt we can do just yet. But keep yer eyes peeled. Ah'm getting the feeling that something's not reet. We might be in for a spot of bother. Ah hope you're handy with your fists," he said, giving Ralph and Jake the once-over.

"Err, well," said Ralph, who had never been in a fight in his life.

"I've done the rounds," said Jake, squaring his shoulders.

Ben nodded. "Thought 'twas so," he said. "It's a good job Ah've come prepared." He drew a flagon out of a saddlebag. "This 'ere's oil. We'll rub the horses all over w'it, so if anyone tries to grab em, they'll have a hard time. It's an owd trick."

The three slicked the horses down with oil.

"Ah'll let you both in on another trick o' the smuggling trade," said Ben. "Ah've trained the 'orses up to bolt when Ah say 'Whoa' and to stop when Ah say 'Gee Up.'" He grinned with satisfaction. "They're good 'orses and the squire makes sure they're well looked after. They can be high-spirited and if they get the chance to have a run around, they will. You think on those commands. The opposite of what to expect. 'Twill be useful if we get ambushed by officers or the villain on the fells. Shout 'Whoa', and the horses will bolt. It'll cause disarray and confusion."

Jake liked that idea. He almost hoped he got a chance to use it. He was learning a lot about the smuggling trade. It was a like chain with each link dependent on the next. And more than enough people ready to find a weakness and break that chain.

Ralph was still recovering from the double shock of his experience in the stone circle and his near arrest. He noticed Jake was giving him some hard looks. He said nothing.

They came to Swinside Farm. A few hens pecked the dirt by a tethered goat. Some farm implements were piled outside the barn door. A cock was crowing but there was no-one to be seen. They walked across the cobbles, not bothering to cover the horses' hooves with rags. It was daylight, after all. A child appeared round a corner but was snatched back by a figure dressed in black, head covered with a shawl. No eye contact was made, and no greeting offered.

Ralph noticed a smell of tobacco lingering in the wintry morning air. The farmer's about, he thought.

They walked through the farmyard and came to a ramshackle barn. There was no door or windows.

"We were going to stop 'ere," said Ben. "But not now. Always good to change things at the last minute. Teks folk off guard. Means we're not so predictable. We'll press on for a bit."

They turned northwards, squelching uphill through some boggy ground. The icy rivulets had melted and there was a series of becks and little waterfalls. They came to a footbridge.

Much use this bridge is, thought Ralph. My feet are already soaked.

"Fenwick's Farm," said Ben. "We'll stop here and rest up for the day. There's a barn yonder."

They led the horses into the barn. Everything was silent. There was a trough of water and, Ralph noticed, a few wrinkled apples in a barrel.

Ben started to unpick an oilskin bag. "We'll leave some baccy out for the farmer," he said. "For the use of his barn and for keeping his mouth shut. Some for Swinside too. They'll expect it and we might need their help. If all goes well, we'll stop here on the way back."

Ralph thought the barn was an obvious place to stop. If he was a preventive officer, it would be exactly the kind of place he would look for smugglers on their way to Frith Hall.

"We're not very well hidden here," he said. "It's on the track. It'll be easy if someone wants to find us." He swallowed and thought of his near arrest. The preventive officer might have got his nerve back, after his scare in the stone circle. He might be on their trail again.

But Ben wasn't concerned. "The farmer at Swinside can see anyone coming from afar," he said. "It's broad daylight. E'll let us know if there's 'owt to be worried aboot. An' we'll be gone by dusk. But to be on safe side, Ah'll keep awake while you get some kip. We'll tek it in turns."

The barn was small, and the horses gave off some heat. Within minutes, Jake and Ralph were asleep.

Chapter Six

'If we advance unstrengthened by repose'

The Duddon Sonnets by William Wordsworth

"Ooof," Ralph was dreaming a horse had pitched him into the middle of the stone circle. The shadows were closing in on him again. "Gerroff," he shouted, arms flailing.

"Ralph, wake up," Jake was shaking him by the shoulders. "Wake up. We've got to get out of here."

"Whassat? Wassamarrer?"

"The farmer sent a message from Swinside to tell us someone is coming. We're off."

Ralph scrambled to his feet. He had a good idea who was coming. The preventive officer had decided to get back on the trail. Maybe he'd gone for help and was planning to arrest all three of them.

Ben was already out of the door. "Follow me now. No time to waste. Not if you want to save yer necks."

Jake and Ralph got their horses. Jake had the presence of mind to kick over the traces of where they slept. Ralph grabbed the last of the withered apples and stuffed them into a saddle bag. They had no chance to talk.

I still haven't asked him what he saw in that circle, Jake thought. Something's going on and I want to know what.

Still groggy from sleep, Ralph stumbled along, keeping pace with Ben's increased speed. Apart from sparse patches of woodland, the fell was very exposed and very boggy. They were bearing north.

"We're going to skirt around this 'ere bog," said Ben. "I know a way that's mostly dry, so follow my footsteps, close as you can. With any luck, whoever's following us will try to tek a short cut and get bogged down. As soon as we get over that slope, we'll be out of sight." Ben strode to the side of the bog with confidence, leading the way.

Jake kept looking back. He could not see anyone following them. They'd had a good start But, he guessed, the pursuer could be on horseback and moving fast.

So far, so good, thought Jake.

I was right, thought Ralph. We should never have stopped at that barn.

We're losing the light, thought Ben. Once in the dark, we're safe.

The smugglers were over the next slope by the time darkness was falling. Ben was guided by the landmarks he knew well. They kept to the track easily.

"Clovenstone," he said in a low voice as they came to a large boulder, cloven into three. "An imprint of the devil's hoof. The devil that pulled down the church. He made his way north after his wicked deed was done."

You're making that up. It's just another one of your stories, thought Ralph but said nothing. The boulder really did look like a cloven hoof.

"We're in the clear lads," said Ben. "Too difficult to find us now it's dark. We haven't heard or seen anything. We'll make Frith Hall just after midnight, by my reckoning."

A few hours later, Ralph thought he could make out the outline of a building on top of the next hill. It looked like there was a candle flickering in the window. We're there, he thought. That's got to be Frith Hall.

Ben halted and walked down the train of pack horses to speak to Ralph. He motioned Jake to join them.

"Yup, we're nearly there. Another hour at most. Ah've timed it so we can finish the drop under cover of darkness. Ah don't know what's happened to whoever was following us, but my guess is that the garn was too difficult in the dark and he gave up. The farmer at Swinside woudn't have helped him, perhaps sent him down the wrong track. But we've still got to be very careful, eh? As long as we've got the contraband in our possession, we could be done for. So, no slip-ups and watch yer step."

Ralph and Jake gave a sigh of relief.

I can't wait to dump this contraband and go home, Ralph thought. I don't care if I do get seasick.

Chapter Seven

'some awful spirit'

The Duddon Sonnets by William Wordsworth

The closer they got to Frith Hall, the more uneasy Ralph became. The building was forbidding and grim. If it had a face, it would look angry, he thought. He remembered Millom Castle. He thought now that the shadow on the steps was the preventive officer. But he'd still felt a hand on his shoulder, and when he'd turned around, no-one was there. He thought about the owl's white face in the darkness. That was natural enough. But a creeping sense of dread persisted. There was all that talk of Ben's about spirits and creatures from another world. It unnerved him. And he could not banish from his mind the haunting memory of what happened in the stone circle. There was no explanation. He was not looking forward to passing Sunkenkirk on the way back.

Ralph shook his head. A plague on Ben and his superstitions! Boggarts and 'obs and the devil's cloven hoof. He'd put all sorts of ideas into Ralph's mind. But, Ralph reasoned, what happened at the stone circle had nothing to do with Ben's superstitions. The preventive officer had seen it too. He'd fled, screaming.

No, Ralph told himself, better be prepared. Anything can happen in this God-forsaken valley.

"The family at Millom Castle used Frith Hall as a hunting lodge," whispered Ben, as they stopped at the bottom of the hill and waited for the signal. "The deer are big round here. But now it's got a bad name.

A lot of fratchin' and fightin'. There was a murder a few months ago. A gruesome one an' all."

"What happened?" asked Jake.

"Some disagreement garn bad," said Ben. "Course, the villain with a mangled hand was involved. Whenivver there's trouble, 'e's there. Nobody can prove he committed murder, but everyone knows he did it. There was an officer of the law there too, can you believe it? But did he turn 'im in? No, he didn't. Said the murder was self-defence. Baloney. It was an innocent traveller, murdered in cold blood. An old woman saw what happened. She knows the truth of the matter, but she canna give witness. Wanders aboot talking rubbish, so they say."

They kept their eyes on Frith Hall, waiting for three candles to be lit, one by one.

"How do they know we're here?" asked Jake, stamping his feet, impatient to be out of the cold night air. Even a draughty barn would be better. "We could have arrived hours ago."

"They dunna," replied Ben. "They're expecting us, but they dunna ken when. So, they keep lighting the signal during each night's waiting. If we're doing our job properly, they dun even know we're here now. But when we've finished unloading, we'll give 'em long low whistle as we're passing the front door. Then they'll know for sure. They'll check the barn as soon as it's daylight and move the goods on."

"Who buys the contraband?" asked Ralph.

"The parson will tek some and hide it in his church for the locals. The hostelry on the other side of the fells might tek some an' all. But most of the liquor stays here. They get through a lot of rum at Frith Hall."

Just when Ralph thought they had been waiting for an eternity and wondering if the signal would ever come, the light of one candle appeared in an upstairs window. Ralph held his breath. Yes, now there were two. And finally, a third candle was lit. There was no mistake; there were three candles, all lit at the same time in the upstairs window.

Ben beckoned Ralph. "Mind the 'orses you two, while I open the barn door. I'll whistle when I'm ready for you to bring 'em in. Be as quiet as you can." Ralph nodded.

Ralph and Jake waited, growing colder by the minute. The horses snorted, their breath making grey clouds in the darkness. The three candles still burned in the upstairs window.

What's keeping him, thought Ralph. Just as he was starting to get worried, he heard a long low whistle. At last. He got hold of the first horse and moved in the direction of the whistle. Jake brought up the rear.

Ralph entered the barn first, followed by the twelve horse and Jake. Straining his eyes, he could see nothing. He wondered if the gang-master's trick of wearing an eye patch was any good. Nothing Ralph had ever tried could make him see in the dark.

He heard a movement.

"Ben?" his whisper was loud. "Ben. Where are you? I can't see a thing."

There was a thud and a groan. Then the sound of the barn door slamming.

"Ben'll not answer you," said a voice.

Ralph felt his stomach drop to his boots.

Chapter Eight

'while men are growing out of boys'

The Duddon Sonnets by William Wordsworth

Whose voice was that? What kind of danger was he in now? What had happened to Ben?

The preventive officer must have outsmarted us, Ralph thought. He's got here first. We've walked into a trap. Ben's probably tied up with a rag stuffed in his mouth. It's the gallows for us now.

Ralph could hear nothing except the swish of horses' tails and their usual noises, a snort, a nicker, a whinny and a fart. He grabbed hold of the nearest horse and laid his cheek against the side of its face, heart thumping. He hoped Jake was doing the same. Then, through his fear, the meaning of the thud and the groan became clear. Jake had been knocked out. Probably lying in the straw with a broken head.

I'm next, Ralph thought. Unless I do something. What good is this - cowering behind a horse? Get a grip, he told himself.

Ralph waited. In the darkness his senses were on full alert. There was an unfamiliar smell of brandy and stale sweat. A shaft of weak moonlight pierced a gap at the top of the barn door. For a brief second, Ralph saw the shadowy outline of a figure, standing with his back to the door, blocking any possibility of escape. It was the motionless figure of a man. Something about the stranger made Ralph begin to doubt it was the preventive officer. Surely, he would have used his authority to arrest Ralph by now, like he did last time. Or tried to. This man didn't seem to be in any hurry, he was biding his time. Something was not right.

Ralph crouched on the floor. He didn't know how big the barn was, or if there were any stalls. He thought there must be a loft, to store hay. He felt his way along the ground, away from the horses, in case they got restless and kicked

"You won't be able to get out of here," said the voice. "I'm coming for you shortly. You'll do as I say."

Ralph did not respond. That would give away his whereabouts. He crept, feeling his way along the straw-covered floor. It had been a while since it was mucked out; Ralph knew he was stinking of horse manure.

He gave a thought to the horses. They snickered and whinnied, expecting water and hay.

Exploring the space in front of him, he came to the wall. He got to his feet and with his back against the wall, shuffled slowly, crab-like, feeling either side with his hands. He knew he must be making some noise, but not enough to be heard above the horses.

Gradually he made his way around the inside of the barn. He felt a sick dread; he knew he must be getting near the door and the scoundrel who had knocked out Jake, and probably Ben too. Then his right hand came across something; a rod, a pole, what was it? Ralph dared to hope it was a ladder to the loft. He felt and found a rung. Yes, there was a loft after all. If he could climb up there perhaps, he would be safe for a while. It would give him time to think of something.

Ralph climbed the first rung of the ladder. It creaked. He held his breath and did not move. Some of the horses became restless and started to stamp. Very slowly, feeling his way, Ralph climbed, hands groping and legs shaking. He could barely swallow. It didn't make any difference if he screwed his eyes shut or stretched them wide; he could not see his hand in front of him. How high was this loft? If he fell now, he would more than likely break his neck. At last, Ralph felt for a rung which was not there. He fumbled for the loft's floor and hoisted himself off the ladder.

Ralph lay on the hay, steadying his breath. Thoughts whirled around his head. If the officer came after him, he could push away the ladder. But then he would be trapped. What could he use to defend himself? Perhaps there was a sickle or a scythe in a corner. He would search in a minute. He hoped the loft floor was sound, so many farm buildings were ramshackle and in need of repair. He did not stand much chance if he fell through the floor from this height. How could he get rid of the man in the barn? Who was it, if it wasn't the preventive officer? How could he help Jake and Ben?

A creak alerted him. He peered over the loft edge. The barn door was opening, and the figure stepped out into the dimmest of moonlight.

Ralph watched. He heard a flint strike against steel and saw a shower of sparks in what would be a tinder box. Of course! The man who held them captive had gone outside for a smoke. No-one would use a tinder box near hay. The barn door was ajar, the figure just in front. Ralph would not be able get past.

But he had the beginnings of a plan.

Chapter Nine

'Who swerves from innocence, who makes divorce
Of that serene companion – a good name,
Recovers not his loss; but walks with shame,
With doubt, with fear, and haply with remorse.'

The Duddon Sonnets by William Wordsworth

Back in the stone circle, when the preventive officer had run off screaming, Ralph had wriggled out of the rope that bound his hands and tied it round his waist. It wasn't thick rope, like they used on the lugger, but a light, slim hemp rope.

He unravelled it from his waist. It wasn't long, about thrice his body length. He guessed the officer planned to tie him to a horse and lead him away down the valley.

I might have been spared capture and prison, reflected Ralph. But right now, I'm hardly any better off.

He slithered to the back of the loft, holding the rope. His hands found a pitchfork under the hay. Just as he expected, the barn was in need of repair and the wood creaked and groaned under his weight. At the end of the loft, he lay on his back and kicked against the wall with both feet. The dried clay and rotten timber cracked and splintered into a hole. Ralph didn't wait to see if he had been heard. He pushed away the ladder, swung the pitchfork outside and then looped the rope over the nearest beam and secured a knot.

Ralph could not trust the strength of the beam, the rope or the knot, but he had no choice. He grabbed the rope with both hands and scaled down the wall. The rope ran out too soon and Ralph was left dangling with no idea how far he would drop.

I hope I'm not going to land on that pitchfork, thought Ralph, letting go. Apart from knocking the breath out of his lungs, the drop was not as bad as he feared. He found the pitchfork and scrambled to his feet. With his back against the wall, he looked for the light from Frith Hall. He would make his way there and get help.

Hardly had he the chance to move when he stopped in his tracks. Was that the mumble of voices? He listened, alert. Yes, he was sure. Ralph edged a little closer, back against the wall, gripping the pitchfork.

"How did you make such a muck up of everything, you corney-faced jackanapes? Hey? Damn your blood but you're useless."

There was a low response, which Ralph did not catch.

"You were supposed to have got rid of them by now." The voice rose in anger. "That was the plan. Get rid of the three of them and bring the goods here. You didn't keep your end of the bargain, so why should I? I've had to do all the work."

"What do you mean, you've done all the work?" said a second voice, rising in alarm. They'd better not be harmed, there's a head price on smugglers."

There was a heavy pause. The first speaker dropped his voice and Ralph strained to hear. "I see it all now," he said, in a tone of voice which sounded a long way from happy understanding. "You weren't going to pay them off with the money I gave you, were you?"

There was no reply. Ralph imagined the second speaker was biting his tongue.

"You weren't going to tell them you'd turn a blind eye if they took the money and ran? You were going to arrest them, weren't you? Arrest them, keep my money and claim the head price when the time comes." The voice, low and threatening, suddenly changed in tone.

"You're nothing but a treacherous, malingering jackanapes." There was scuffle, the sound of a thump, then choking and spluttering.

"I'm here, aren't I? The goods are here," the second voice gasped. "Nothing's amiss. We can still deal with the smugglers."

There was another bout of coughing followed by wheezing and groaning.

"I had him; I swear." The second voice was pleading. "I'd got him on the ground, got him tied up. Oh, but he called the spirits on me, he did. If I tell you what happened, what I saw, you wouldn't believe me. Put the frighteners on me, it did, God help me. I had to let him go."

"Called the spirits on you? You're right, I don't believe it. What d'ya take me for, you fat-headed stink matter? When I see those smugglers gibbeted and dangling, I'll collect the head price myself. You've done naught, so you get naught. And I'll have my money back now, before I throttle you 'til your tongue's as black as this night sky."

There was the sound of another thump and more gasping. Ralph almost felt sorry for the preventive officer, for no doubt it was the same man who had attempted to arrest him in Sunkenkirk stone circle.

So, thought Ralph, the preventive officer had been bribed. He was supposed to bribe us and send us on our way. But he didn't. Tried to arrest us instead. Well, that little plan backfired. Ralph knew that the revenue service was full of idleness and corruption. The preventive officer would not be the first to succumb to bribery. But he would be regretting it now.

"When day breaks, we'll have to get rid of all three of them. Your fault, since you didn't tell them to scarper. Where's the nearest well, you chunk of useless nothing?"

"HHHodge Wife Well," stammered the preventive officer. "Over by Mere Crag. Why?"

"Why do you think?" was the dark reply.

Chapter Ten

'after theft
Of some sweet babe, flower stolen, and coarse weed left
For the distracted mother to assuage
Her grief with, as she might!'

The Duddon Sonnets by William Wordsworth

Ralph had heard enough. Come morning, he didn't give much for their chances. He thought the preventive officer should be worried too. He needed to get help from Frith Hall as soon as he could.

The three candles were still burning in the window, the sign that the way was clear for the drop off. Little did they know.

Ralph hurried to the front door and opened it. The passageway led to a large room, scattered with several tables and stools. Dying embers in a large fireplace gave a dull yellow light. A candle lantern burned in the hearth. At first, he thought the room was empty, but then he heard a creak of a chair and made out the figure of an old woman.

She studied him with tiny, unblinking eyes. Her claw-like hands gripped the sides of a rocking chair.

As Ralph approached, she leaned forward. "Did you see them?" she asked, wheezing. "They stole my baby and left a changeling. I brought him up as my own son, I did, but he's bad, so bad. He did a very bad thing." She covered her face with her hands. "Every night I seek my own baby, the one they took away. Where did they take him? Do you know?" She started to whimper.

The soul's demented, thought Ralph, guessing she might be the old woman Ben mentioned. She's no good to me.

"I need to speak to the landlord of this establishment," he said, addressing the old woman with an air of firm authority that surprised him. Suddenly he felt more confident. He had got out of the barn and away from that villain. Now he must rescue Ben and Jake. It was not too late.

"Tell me where I can find the landlord. It's a matter of urgency."

The old woman's sad eyes looked at Ralph's face, but she was not listening.

"Begone, you old bag of rags." Behind the voice strode a man from the corner of the room. His appearance startled Ralph. He had not been aware there was anyone else in the room. The man was pale of face and broad of shoulder. He held a walking cane.

The old woman shrieked. "You! William Marshall! How did you manage to come back?"

"Not through any help from you," the man snarled. He opened his jacket, revealing a long wound across his chest, still fresh. "Do you remember how I came by this, you worthless old crone?"

The old woman clutched at her hair and let out a long wail. It was a fearful sound.

I wish she'd shut up, thought Ralph, I've been vexed enough for one night.

As if she could read his thoughts, the old woman got up from her chair and stumbled from the dark room.

"Good riddance," said the man after her.

Ralph became impatient with this strange exchange. He needed to go back to the barn and get Jake and Ben before they were thrown down Hodge Wife Well.

"It's sorry news I bring, landlord," Ralph said. "The contraband is in the stable but not for long. We've been set upon by some villain and a scheming preventive officer. I need your help. My two companions are held captive

56

and silenced. T'will go badly for them if we do not go to their aid before the night's end. Will you help?"

"I vow I know this villain," said the man with the wound on his chest. "But let him cast his eyes on one William Marshall and see how he fares then. Come." He grabbed the candle lantern from the hearth, beckoned Ralph and they strode through the front door towards the barn.

There was no sign of the two men. The barn door was ajar.

"I challenge you to come outside and look me in the face," said William Marshall, holding the cane in one hand and swinging the lantern in the other. They stood in front of the doorway,

"Come out, you rotten lousy murdering thief."

As the light swung in an arc, they saw a man emerge from the barn. With his left hand he was holding Jake's collar. And with his right hand he was holding a knife to Jake's throat. A right hand with no fingertips.

Chapter Eleven

'Was the intruder nursed
In hideous usages, and rites accursed,
That thinned the living and disturbed the dead?'

The Duddon Sonnets by William Wordsworth

This is the man who wants to throw us all down Hodge Wife Well, thought Ralph. I might have guessed.

About time you showed up, thought Jake. This villain knocked me out and now he's got a knife to my throat. Get me out of here!

Where is Ben? thought Ralph. And the preventive officer? What do we do now?

William Marshall stood his ground. He seemed unconcerned to see a young boy held hostage, with a knife to his throat. He held his cane aloft in one hand and brought the lantern closer to his face.

"Get the horses and start leading them out, you sad excuse for a preventive officer," the man holding Jake said, over his shoulder. "I'll deal with this lot." He leered at Jake, prodding the knife into his neck.

Then he lifted his head and and looked at William Marshall.

The preventive officer took the first horse's reins. "Gee up," he said, expecting the horse to move forwards. The horse remained still. "Gee up," he repeated, tugging at the reins. Still the horse did not move. The preventive officer gave the horse a shove. His hands slipped where the horse had been oiled and he lost his balance, falling flat on his face in a pile of steaming horse manure. He got up, said nothing but expecting a torrent of abuse. Then he noticed. His fellow thief was motionless, unable to wrench his eyes from the face in front of him. The face of William Marshall.

The preventive officer followed his gaze. He saw William Marshall's features illuminated by the lantern's flickering light. He too stopped in his tracks. The horse's reins fell from his hands and he sank to his knees. To Ralph's astonishment, the preventive officer started uttering frantic prayers to the Almighty.

The man with chopped-off fingers was transfixed by the sight of William Marshall. Jake felt the grip on his collar loosen.

It was all he needed. Breaking away, Jake ran through the barn shouting as hard as he could.

"Whoa! Whoa, I say. Whoa!" With every 'whoa' he clapped his hands.

The horses took fright, neighing and whinnying. Ralph opened the barn door as wide as it would go. "Whoa!" he joined in. "Whoa!"

Still laden with contraband, the horses bolted. The rum, brandy, tea and tobacco disappeared into the night. The rogue gave himself a shake and the preventive officer a vicious kick. Then greed overcame fear, and he ran into the dark winter's night, after the horses.

"Stop! Whoa! Whoa! You stupid beasts, Whoa!"

Jake laughed, easing his collar away from his neck. "The more he says 'Whoa', the more they'll run."

He turned to the preventive officer, still on his knees, gibbering. "Get out of here and don't come back, if you know what's good for you."

The officer scrambled to his feet and looked at Ralph. "You consort with the devil," he gabbled. "You raise spirits from the dead. That face… in the stone circle… William Marshall… here…"

"I said 'Get out!' Jake clenched his fists.

Ralph, still holding the pitchfork, prodded the preventive officer none too gently.

"You heard." Prod. "Get out." Prod. "And don't ever show your face to us again." Double prod. The preventive officer scurried out of the barn, falling over his feet.

"And where were you when I was knocked out by that villain? I thought it was the end, when I saw him with that knife." Jake asked. He gave Ralph a friendly punch, for in fact he was greatly relieved to see his friend.

"I escaped from the barn and got help from Frith Hall. We're in debt of our lives to William Marshall here."

William Marshall stepped forward. He handed Ralph his walking cane. "My night's work is over," he said. "Give this to your gang-master and tell him William Marshall has no further need of it." Ralph took the cane and examined it. He saw that it had a silver top, the kind a gentleman would use. It was an unusual thing to see in a remote valley, far away from well-dressed gentlemen and life in the town.

They heard a moan coming from the corner of the barn. Ralph took the lantern from William Marshall and found Ben in a corner. There was a wound on his temple and his face was caked in blood.

"We may as well spend what's left of the night at Frith Hall," said Jake, helping Ben to his feet, "and get you cleaned up. "The horses have bolted and we'll never find them in the dark. And I have no wish to bump into that bad-tempered villain again."

In spite of his sore head, Ben chuckled. "Never thee mind," he said. "The 'orses are trained to go back to the squire. Ah'm wagering that scoundrel will never catch up wi'em, blast his eyes. Ah ken 'e was aboot, when Ah saw that smoke. We're lucky to be still alive."

Ben staggered, still dizzy from the blow on his head. Ralph and Jake guided him towards the barn doorway. All was quiet at Frith Hall. There was no sign of William Marshall. The old woman had gone too.

The next day, the three made their way back down the valley. Some bread and apples had been left on a flat stone by Swinside Farm.

"The goodly folk 'ere ken what we've suffered," said Ben. "It's their way of aiding us."

Progress was quicker in the daylight. As they passed Sunkenkirk, Ralph looked with curiosity, but unafraid. There were no moving shadows or uncanny faces on vibrating rocks.

After they passed the old castle, they were ready to bid farewell to Ben and join the ship.

"All that for nothing," said Ralph. "We got the contraband to Frith Hall, but the horses made off with it again. At least that rogue's plans came to nothing. But it won't go down well with the gang-master. I'm not looking forward to telling him."

"Never fret yersels. Tell thy gang-master that the squire will keep contraband safe and git word aboot. Contraband and folk will find each other, never fear. But tell me, 'ow did you come by that silver-topped cane in yer 'and? I never saw it going up the valley."

'William Marshall said to give it to the gang-master," said Ralph. "You never saw him. You were out cold. By the time you'd come to, he'd gone. But he saved us. We owe him a debt of gratitude."

"William Marshall, ye say?" Ben's eyes glinted and he nodded. "Aye, William Marshall. 'So, 'e had a hand in all this. I might a ken. "He'll be back wi' the 'obs and boggarts by now."

Well, that blow on the head didn't knock any sense into him, thought Ralph. Still going on about 'obs and boggarts.

Chapter Twelve

'Truth's holy lamp'

The Duddon Sonnets by William Wordsworth

Ralph and Jake were glad of the prospect of sailing home. They waded through the surf and joined the ship. They decided to tell the gang-master everything. And, for the first time, Jake heard what happened to Ralph in the stone circle.

"So, Ben says the contraband will be safe in the Squire's keeping," said Ralph, anxious about the gang-master's reaction.

"Squire's got word to me," said the gang-master. "He's told me that the contraband is safe. I know I can trust him. And now I know that I can trust you too."

These were gracious words indeed from the gang-master. Ralph and Jake were hugely relieved.

"There's something else," said Ralph. "William Marshall, the man who saved us at Frith Hall, said to give you this. Says he has no further need of it." Ralph handed over the cane.

The gang-master pushed his eye patch onto his forehead, took the cane and examined it carefully.

"So, William Marshall is the name of the man who helped you?" he asked. "I heard he frequents the place. This cane proves it then."

"He saved us," said Ralph again. "Without him, we would be at the bottom of Hodge Wife Well. And the contraband would be gone for good."

"How did he look?"

"Well, actually, he was wounded," said Ralph. "On his chest. Didn't seem to bother him though. You know him then?"

"Like a brother." The gang-master shrugged. "I suppose you've heard the stories about me. Switched at birth and all that. They say I was born somewhere in the Duddon Valley. That it's a place of bad goings-on and mischievous spirits. Well, you've brought back tales of boggarts and haunted stone circles and such like, so maybe it is. Anyway, the story goes that the spirits took me away from my real mother and brought me to the Isle of Man. Left a foundling baby in my place. Not sure I believe it myself."

Ralph remembered the old woman clutching his arm and gibbering about her baby being taken. "I can believe it," he said.

The gang-master raised his eyebrows. "Still interrupting me, aren't you?" he said. "It's not your place to say, though, is it? I'm not interested in what you believe."

Ralph bristled but said nothing.

"Anyway, left my mother with a foundling from the spirit world they did," he continued. "That's the story. I heard the baby they left her with turned out bad ways, although his mother, my mother, did her best. I was brought to the Isle of Man and William Marshall's family adopted me. We grew up together. Of course, we both went into the smuggling trade". He looked at the silver-topped cane. "One day it took him to Frith Hall." A pause. "He never came back."

"Why? What happened?" Jake ventured to ask. Ralph remained silent.

The gang-master drew a deep breath. "Some time ago," he said. "On a run to Scotland, I was given this silver-topped cane as part payment for a keg of rum. A parson, it was. I had no use for it, so I gave it to William. He took it everywhere. Liked to joke around, pretending to be a gentleman, he did." The gang-master smiled at the memory.

"One day he had to take some goods to Frith Hall. Of course, he took the cane with him. But it brought him attention he didn't want. There was an argument. A local mean-spirited ruffian picked a fight. Said William must have stolen the cane. Called him a common thief and other names. Of course, it was that villain with no fingertips."

A sad look came into the gang-master's eyes. He drew down the eye patch. "William was never one to keep his temper. It got him into many a scrape. But Frith Hall was an ugly fight. The scoundrel had a knife and William was murdered. He's been dead a while."

Ralph stared. He started to realise what the gang-master was saying. This must be the murder that Ben had spoken about.

"But" he spoke, forgetting himself, "we saw him. He spoke to us."

"You didn't see William Marshall. You saw his ghost. He was looking out for me, his brother. He always did."

"He spoke to an old woman too," Ralph suddenly remembered.

An old woman, you say," the gang-master showed interest. "I heard an old woman saw the fight, saw what happened. But she won't speak out. She talks gibberish, so she can't be made to give evidence. And poor William cannot rest until justice is done. I've heard he haunts the place."

The gang-master studied the cane again. "I'm going to find that villain one day soon. He'll get what's coming to him. And then William can rest in peace."

Ralph was silent. So, it was true then. About spirits from another world.

Then he understood. The foundling left by the spirit world, who grew up to do a bad thing. The man with the chopped off fingers. The murderer of William Marshall. They were one and the same person.

There was something else too. Maybe, Ralph thought, if the gang-master goes to Frith Hall to avenge his brother's death, he will meet the old woman. Then he would get to know the truth.

Meanwhile, it wasn't his place to say.

Footnote

Frith Hall is thought to have been built about 1608 and may have succeeded Ulpha Old Hall as a Hunting Lodge for the Hudlestons of Millom Castle.

The Hudleston family supported the King and so the defeat by Parliamentary forces in the Civil Wars (1642-1651) meant the family's ruin. As Ben said, Millom Castle was damaged by cannon fire in 1644.

Frith Hall then ceased to be a hunting lodge and became a hostelry. Runaway marriages were reported to have taken place there and it became a place of bad reputation. The death of William Marshall in 1736 is thought to be the result of a drunken altercation or a murder. He is said to be buried nearby and of course his ghost haunts the building.

Frith Hall then became a farm but is now a crumbling ruin and can be seen on the skyline of Ulpha fells.

From the days of the Cistercian monks of Furness Abbey, wool was a source of income for many. Ralph's route to Frith Hall would have been used by pack horses carrying wool as well as smuggled goods.

SEATHWAITE
1904-1911

'No record tells of lance opposed to lance,
Horse charging horse'

The Duddon Sonnets by William Wordsworth

William Wordsworth reportedly visited the Newfield Inn, in the remote and peaceful village of Seathwaite. He writes that there is no record of battles having taken place in the Duddon Valley.

But later, during the years 1904-1911 Seathwaite was the scene of rioting, killing, explosions, violent deaths and horrific injuries. News of these events spread far and wide. This selection of newspaper articles tells the stories which begin in the 'heat-oprest' summer of 1904.

'Mid-noon is past; - upon the sultry mead
No zephyr breathes, no cloud its shadow throws:'

The Duddon Sonnets by William Wordsworth

Sunderland Daily Echo and Shipping
Gazette Thursday 28th July 1904

The Seathwaite Riot

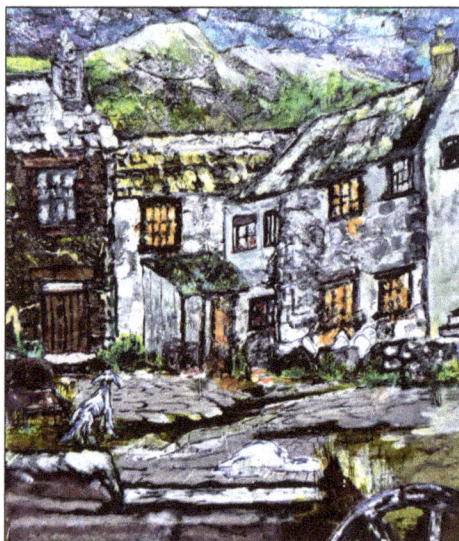

Yesterday there was a restoration of some of the calm in the Duddon Valley, but despite the restoration of quietness there were two sequels which bore their melancholy evidence of the tragedy which resulted in the death of the Millom labourer, Owen Cavanagh. One was at Ulverston, the centre of the North Lonsdale police area, which probably ranks among the largest in the Kingdom, and the other at Seathwaite, the scene of the tragedy.

At Ulverston, Thomas Dawson landlord of the Newfield Hotel, Seathwaite, a grey-bearded man of the farming type, who is alleged to have shot down James Foy, and James Greenhow, a medium built young fellow, who acted as barman at the hotel, and is stated to have defended the house against the attack of the ruffians by shooting Garrett Kinsella, and Henry Knox Todd, another young fellow who has been acting as an assistant engineer at the Seathwaite Tarn dam construction for the firm of Messers Kennedy Limited of Glasgow, and who, it is alleged, fired the shot which killed Cavanagh, were each placed in the dock. Two solicitors, Mr Butler of Broughton, representing Dawson and Greenhow and Mr Bradshaw of Barrow, representing Todd, were present, and Mr John Coward, of Ulverston was the magistrate.

The charges of unlawfully wounding against Dawson and Greenhow, and of causing the death of Cavanagh against Todd, were taken separately, although only one witness was called.

The police court story was of a thrilling nature because it brought a description from a person who witnessed the terrible attack on Seathwaite Church and schools and on the hotel and its occupants.

Cumberland Pacquet July 28th 1904

Supt Whitaker of Ulverston and a strong force of police arrived on the scene in the evening and the district is being scoured for the remaining rioters, whose number is estimated at 9.

One of those who fled was known to be wounded in the hand and another arrested at Millom on Thursday. 3 persons were arrested at Coniston for participation in the riot and were supposed to have crossed Walna Scar Pass.

One of the rioters still at large is hiding amongst the mountains in the vicinity of Wasdale Head and occasionally sallying forth to neighbouring houses in search of food.

Thomas Dawson was remanded for a fortnight.

Sunderland Daily Echo and Shipping Gazette
Wednesday 17th August 1904

The Seathwaite Riot

Verdict of 'Justifiable Homicide'

The adjourned inquest was held yesterday at Seathwaite on the body of Owen Cavanagh who was shot during a riot of navvies at a public house about three weeks ago.

The evidence showed that a man named Foy was going to sleep in the bar, when the landlord told him he must get out. A dispute followed, and Foy was joined by Kinsella, Cavanagh and Burns and other navvies. The landlord was threatened with his life and the men broke every window with stones and smashed up the bar. They afterwards went away, and broke the windows of the church and school, and then returned to the public house.

The landlord and his assistants were in the kitchen, and hearing the men coming, seized some shotguns. The navvies made a rush, and a barman named John Greenhow fired and shot Kinsella, while another man, Henry Todd fired at Cavanagh. The landlord was attacked by Foy and shot him likewise. Cavanagh died the following day from his wounds.

A witness said the rioters threatened to murder everyone in the house even if they swung for it. He did not know why the men smashed the windows of the church.

Henry Todd, who shot Cavanagh, told the coroner that he did not intend to kill the deceased. He only wanted to disable him, as he was just then in the act of hurling a large stone through the window. He shot as low as he could, but Cavanagh was in a crouching position at the time.

The jury returned a verdict of Justifiable Homicide.

The Chairman of the Bench addressed James Greenhow;

'The law which as applied to this case appears to be that only such force as is necessary to preserve the property or lives of persons is justifiable, and therefore of necessity firearms are only to be used as a last resource. Having regard to the number of persons who were assailing your master's property, to their violence and the threats made against the lives of your mistress, yourself and others in the house, and to all the facts of the case, the Bench cannot say that you were not justified in what you did, and therefore you will be discharged.'

Next was Henry Todd

'Henry Knox Todd, the facts of the law in this case are the same as in the case of Greenhow, with three differences.
First, that you were not in the employ of Dawson and therefore it was not your master's property or your mistress that you were defending, and therefore the law requires greater caution on your part; secondly, the man you shot has died from his wounds inflicted by you, and these facts might have caused the Bench to take a different view of your case from that of Greenhow but for a third fact, which was that the deceased and others continued their assault on the house after Kinsella was shot, and therefore we are of the opinion that no jury would convict you, therefore you will be discharged.'

In view of the result of the previous two cases, the Superintendent withdrew the charges and Thomas Dawson was dismissed by the Court.

Sheffield Daily Telegraph 7th November 1904

At Lancaster Assizes on Saturday, Garrett Kinsella, labourer, pleaded guilty to riotous conduct at Seathwaite on July 25th. A riot arose through some navvies being refused more drink at the Newfield Inn and much damage was done in the village. The occupants of the inn fired on the rioters, with the result that a man named Cavanagh was killed and Kinsella and a man named Foy were injured. Justice Phillimore said that Foy and the prisoner had brought serious punishment upon themselves; but for this he would have sent him to penal servitude. A sentence of 9 months hard labour was passed.

Manchester Courier and Lancashire General Advertiser 14th January 1905

At Ulverston yesterday James Foy appeared in the dock with crutches minus the lower half of his left leg after being in hospital for 22 weeks.

Western Times 27th January 1905

At Lancaster Assizes James Foy pleaded guilty to rioting.

Justice Wills said that Foy had been sufficiently punished, sentenced him to 1 day's imprisonment and ordered to return to hospital.

Manchester Courier and Lancashire General Advertiser 30th November 1905

At North Lonsdale Magistrates' Court yesterday James Burns and Thomas Burns were placed in the dock on a charge of rioting at Seathwaite on 25th July 1904.

Supt Whitaker said that the police had scoured the countryside for the two men. Thomas Burns gave himself up to Newcastle police and James Burns was arrested at Askam the previous day. Both the men, who looked poor and haggard, were remanded for a week.

Millom Gazette 19th April 1906

An Echo of the Seathwaite Riot

At Whitehaven on Thursday, James Foy, labourer, Millom, was charged with begging at Bransty, Whitehaven on Wednesday, the case having been proved by P.C. Nixon. The prisoner told the magistrates that he had been waiting at Whitehaven for a letter from South Africa with a trifle in it and intended to go to Millom to get a pedlar's certificate. Supt Hope said the prisoner, who had only one leg, was the ringleader of the riot at Seathwaite and had lost his leg as a result of a gunshot wound received at the time of the riot. The prisoner promised to return to Millom if the bench allowed him to go. Discharged on that understanding.

Millom Gazette 12th March 1909

Explosion at Seathwaite. A landlord shockingly injured

A serious explosion is reported to have occurred on Friday morning at Seathwaite, whereby Thomas Dawson, the well-known landlord of the Newfield Hotel, sustained shocking injuries. Detailed particulars are not to hand, but it is cited that Dawson was engaged in some blasting work with dynamite when a charge which had missed fire suddenly exploded with such terrible force that one of his arms was blown off, part of his face blown away and an eye destroyed. His son was working with him at the time and he was also seriously injured. Word of the accident was sent to Dr Fawcett at Broughton who hurried to the scene.

Newfield Hotel will be vividly remembered by many as the scene, a few years ago, of the famous Seathwaite riot in which a number of men made an attack on the Newfield.

Millom Gazette 19th March 1909

We regret to learn that Mr Dawson, of Newfield, is now totally blind. He has had his left eye taken out and the sight of his other is destroyed as a result of the explosion.

Two years later, Messers Kennedy and Co and the Duddon Waterworks were involved, albeit indirectly, in another violent incident with fatal consequences when two Millom men were killed. In a quarry at the Seathwaite Beck end of the Tarn, an unexploded charge of gelignite was struck, causing a fearsome explosion. Dr Fawcett was called again to a scene of violent death and shocking injury in a backdrop of beauty and tranquillity. William Rodgers, an experienced foreman of the quarrymen for Messers Kennedy and Co, was unable to explain how the unexploded material happened to be there. No blame was attached to the foreman or the employers and the verdict was Accidental Death.

Footnote

The Millom Gazette reported that within a few days of the riot in 1904, the hot weather broke and there were violent thunderstorms up and down the valley. Trees were uprooted and vegetation was damaged. Three people were struck by lightning. Later that summer, a bumper crop of corn was reported.

Initially, the press mistakenly attributed the riot to the presence of navvies, who had come to the Duddon valley to construct a reservoir. However, despite the navvies' previous reputation for rioting, on this occasion they were not involved or responsible. The press subsequently apologised for 'maligning honest folk'.

Foy, Kinsella and Cavanagh were local men from Millom. Cavanagh, who lost his life in the riot, was a young man who had been discharged from the Army as a result of an eye infection.

9 781913 898083